THE STORY OF CAPTAIN SCOTT

This edition published 2025
by Living Book Press

ISBN: 978-1-76153-951-0 (hardcover)
          978-1-76153-923-7 (softcover)

First published in 1920.

This edition is based on the printing by TC & EC Jack.

A catalogue record for this book is available from the National Library of Australia

THE STORY OF CAPTAIN SCOTT

by

MARY MACGREGOR

THE DOGS WERE TAKEN OUT AND HARNESSED TO A SLEDGE

CONTENTS

CHAPTER I

THE TERRA NOVA LEAVES LYTTELTON

"HAD we lived," wrote Captain Scott, in his last message to the public, "I should have had a tale to tell of the hardihood, endurance, and courage of my companions which would have stirred the heart of every Englishman."

Although Scott did not live to tell the tale of the heroism of those who followed him so loyally, he wrote in his journal enough to thrill the heart not only of every Englishman, but of everyone who reads. And the journal which records the bravery and the endurance of his companions, tells us unawares of the strength, the unwavering courage of their leader.

It is the story of Scott's expedition to the South Pole which I am going to tell in this little book. It is a sad story of a brave adventure.

First of all you will wish to know something

about Scott before he became one of our greatest explorers.

Robert Falcon Scott was born in Devonport in June 1868. When he was thirteen years old he became a naval cadet on board the *Britannia*. Two years afterwards, he was a midshipman and served on different ships and at different stations until he was nineteen. In 1889 he reached the rank of lieutenant. A year or two later, he entered a schoolship to study the duties of a torpedo lieutenant. Soon after this, he was made staff officer on the *Defiance*, a torpedo schoolship stationed at Devonport, his own early home.

When Scott was twenty-eight years old, he went to sea as torpedo lieutenant of a battleship. In about a year, he was removed to the *Majestic*, the flagship of the Channel Squadron. One of the admirals under whom he served on the flagship was Sir Henry Stephenson, who had been an explorer in the Arctic regions when his lieutenant was seven years of age.

In June 1900, Scott was promoted to the rank of Commander. It was now that he left the Royal Navy for a time to become an explorer in the Antarctic regions.

The voyage of the *Discovery*, in which ship he sailed on his first expedition, has been told by Scott in a book which you will read for yourself some day.

His return to England in 1904 was a great event. The gallant explorer was feted by societies, honoured by universities. King Edward created him C.V.O., which letters stand for the words Commander of the Victorian Order. In London, a great meeting was held by the Royal Geographical Society at which he was awarded a Royal Medal, and also a special one to commemorate the expedition.

In 1906, Scott was again at sea, but three years later he resigned his appointment that he might prepare for his last great expedition to the South Pole. His object was not only to reach the Pole, but to carry farther the scientific work which had been begun on his first voyage.

In November 1910, the *Terra Nova*, the ship which had been fitted out for the expedition, reached New Zealand. She was leaking badly, so as soon as she arrived at Lyttelton Harbour, she was overhauled. The leak, which was found in the stern of the vessel, was repaired. Water still made its way into the ship, but to keep it under it was necessary now to use only a hand pump for a short time twice a day.

Meanwhile, the stores had been taken out of the ship and were being marked plainly and repacked, so that no time would be wasted when the South was reached.

The men packed with skill gained by practice.

Tents, sledges, provisions, and scientific instruments were stowed away. When this was done, no small part of the men's quarters had been invaded. But the men were so eager for the success of the expedition that they were ready to endure any discomfort.

To provide stalls for the nineteen ponies, to find space for the thirty-three dogs that were going South, was no easy task. Fifteen stalls were built under the forecastle, while four more were placed on the port side of the vessel.

The dogs were perhaps better off than the ponies, for they were chained on deck. All the dogs were Siberian, except two, and they were Esquimaux. Most of the animals had been given to the expedition by schools in England and Scotland. They had been brought across Siberia by Meares, who was to have charge of them on the southern journey. Demetri Gerof had been engaged as dog driver, and had helped Meares in his task, which had been no easy one.

There was an ice-house on board in which large stores of mutton and beef, sweetbreads and kidneys were packed. Scott wished to supply his men with fresh meat as long as possible, as that would help to keep them strong. Bags of coal, cases of petrol, bales of fodder, as well as the things of which I have already told you, and many more which I have not mentioned, were packed away, until every corner of the ship was loaded.

On the 26th November 1910 all was ready, and the *Terra Nova* set sail from Lyttelton Harbour, followed by tugs crowded with friends and well-wishers.

Three days later Scott joined the ship at Port Chalmers. The sun was shining as she left the harbour, surrounded by even more boats and tugs than at Lyttelton. For about two hours they followed the vessel, then slowly and sadly the boats turned back, while the ship sailed on alone.

CHAPTER II

THE STORM

BEFORE a week was over, the *Terra Nova* was tossing on a stormy sea. The ponies in their cramped stalls suffered more than the men, as the ship rolled and pitched before the wind. Again and again in his journal Scott wrote of what the ponies and the dogs had to endure. He told how by looking through a hole in the bulkhead one could see "a row of heads with sad, patient eyes come swinging up together from the starboard side, whilst those on the port swing back; then up come the port heads, while the starboard recede."

But although they suffered, the ponies still ate well. They slept standing, for there was not room to lie down. This was not a hardship, as horses have in each leg a ligament which supports their weight.

The dogs, as I told you, were chained on deck, and during the storm the waves which were constantly breaking over the ship drenched them until they looked poor, miserable creatures. While the storm raged, Oates and Atkinson, two of the officers, did all they could for the comfort of the beasts. A strange thing befell one of the ponies, for a wave of unusual strength snapped his chain and swept him overboard, while the next wave lifted the animal and dropped him again on deck. He must have been a hardy little pony, for he recovered from the shock in a very short time.

Forage cases, petrol cases, instrument cases — all were in danger of serious damage from loose bags of coal which the waves lifted and dashed heedlessly down among them. The men were ordered to the waist of the ship to throw overboard the coal sacks and to try to lash the cases together. It was difficult work, for the men themselves were in danger of being washed away by the heavy seas that broke over them, and they were often forced to stop and cling to anything they could find for safety.

Bad as all this was, it was nothing to the blow that followed. It was found that the pumps in the engine-room were choked. Lashly, the chief stoker, stood up to his neck in water trying vainly to get them clear. But in spite of all his efforts, the water grew deeper and deeper until it reached the boiler.

With the engine-room flooded and heavy seas sweeping the deck, it seemed that the ship must founder. Nothing could be done except, as a last hope, to bale out the water with buckets. The men worked with a will, in shifts of two hours, and at length, after a day and a night of constant peril, the water began to decrease. At the same time the gale blew less fiercely, and although the engine fires were still out and the ship was tossing helplessly from side to side, the danger gradually grew less.

Soon after this, E. Evans, the second in command, found his way to the choked pump, and going down the shaft cleared out the coal and oil that had choked it. The pump was then once more in working order, and the water was kept under without difficulty. So the engine fires were lighted, and the ship sailed away toward the South.

During the storm two ponies died, and one dog was washed overboard.

Osman, the leader of the dog team, was also nearly lost. But after being covered in hay for twenty-four hours, during which time he ate nothing, he began to recover. In another twenty-four hours, he was as well as ever.

The loss of the animals was serious, and perhaps almost as grave was the loss of tons of coal and cases of petrol which had had to be thrown overboard.

While the storm lasted, the men had not spared themselves. They had been drenched to the skin, the mess deck had been streaming with water, there was nothing that had not been jostled out of its place. Yet not only was there no complaint, but the sound of songs and of laughter was heard coming from their quarters.

It was little wonder that Scott had nothing but praise for the conduct of his men.

CHAPTER III

THE ICE-PACK

THE TERRA NOVA was caught in the midst of an ice-pack:

This pack was formed of ice which had frozen the winter before on the edge of the Antarctic Continent, of heavy old ice-floes which had broken out of bays and inlets in summer but had not got far north before another winter had begun, as well as of heavy and thin ice which had formed over the Ross Sea at different times.

There are three ways by which a ship can get through a pack. It can break the pieces of ice — or ice-floes, as these pieces are called — it can push them out of the way if they are not too large, or it can sail round them.

Sometimes the floes are so close together that it seems as though months may pass before a ship can get through the pack; yet, perhaps in an hour, a gap of a foot or more may have been made by the wind. If there are several of these gaps, a ship can soon push its way forward.

From about the middle of December until after Christmas, the *Terra Nova* was struggling to get out of the pack it had encountered. It was the uncertainty of what might happen from hour to hour that made the demand on Scott's patience so great.

Sometimes the ship would succeed in pushing her way through the floes in a zigzag course for an hour or two. Then she would stop entirely, having run into a belt of big floes. If she stopped, the engine-room fires were, when it was possible, allowed to go out to save coal. While the ship was anchored, the officers put on their ski shoes and went off to practise skiing on the large floes. They were so hungry after the unaccustomed exercise that the cook despaired of satisfying their hunger.

Later in the day, ski shoes were given to the men, and Gran, the ski expert, gave them lessons in their use.

Then the dogs were taken out and harnessed to a sledge. They had grown fat without exercise, although their one meal each day consisted of two and a half biscuits. At first, they panted as they ran and did not seem to enjoy the new experience.

There was bird life and fish life all around the ship, so the men had much to interest and amuse them while they were wedged in among the floes. Of the birds, none were so amusing as the penguins,

He would go to one of the floes and lie flat and quite still.

with their quaint movements and curious ways. On land or on ice, they were not only awkward but absurd. In water, they were beautiful, as they dived and darted under the surface or leaped for a moment through the air before again falling into the sea.

Wilson, the doctor on board, used to try to capture some of these birds. He would go to one of the floes and lie there flat and quite still. As the penguins were inquisitive birds, they came with their ludicrous, jerky gait towards the strange object they saw upon the floe. But when they were quite close, they suddenly turned and flapped along in the other direction. Sometimes he would sing to them, and that never failed to attract them, but the moment he stopped they were off and away to their own haunts.

The crew soon learned that the penguins listened to singing, and Scott often laughed as he heard a group of men on the poop singing nonsense rhymes. The audience, he knew, was a group of fascinated penguins.

Scott admired the spirit of his men during these trying weeks. "Everyone is wonderfully cheerful; there is laughter all day long," he wrote in his journal. And the kindliness of each to the other delighted him. "I have not heard a harsh word or seen a black look," was the tribute he paid them.

Christmas Eve came while the ship was still unable to move. Great as Scott's patience was, his journal showed how anxious the delay made him, because of the extra coal that was used when the ship was at a standstill or moving slowly among the floes. "Oh, but it's mighty trying to be delayed and delayed like this and coal going all the time," he wrote.

In spite of everything, Christmas was a happy day. There was service in the morning, to which everyone went, and the heartiness with which the men sang showed that they were there with good-will in their hearts.

There was a dinner of many courses, ending with plum pudding and mince pies. The meal lasted for an hour, while for five hours afterwards the party sat round the table singing songs.

At length, on the 30th of December, Scott was able to write, "We are out of the pack at length and at last," and beneath the words we catch a glimpse of the terrible strain to which his patience had been put.

In a few days, everyone hoped to reach Cape Crozier, which Scott wished to make his base or chief station; but before the Cape was reached, the ship was caught in a blizzard. Little progress could be made, for it blew right in their teeth.

The ponies again suffered greatly from the violence of the storm, and Scott was as distressed as ever over the misery they endured.

"I begin to wonder if fortune will ever turn her wheel," he wrote. "On every possible occasion she seems to have decided against us."

CHAPTER IV

THE *TERRA NOVA* UNLOADED

ON New Year's Eve, the *Terra Nova* was in Ross Sea. "It was a horrible night," wrote Scott, who slept little, thinking, as he did always in a storm, of the misery of the ponies.

The wind was blowing hard, and loose ice-floes were floating about, full of danger to the ship. It was only with difficulty that she was guided behind a solid mass of floes, where she was sheltered from the wind.

Before the year ended, all on board were cheered by the sight of land. For the storm clouds lifted, and far away in the west, the peaks of two great mountains were seen.

The New Year was only a few days old when the ship approached Cape Crozier, where Scott hoped to winter. To his disappointment, he found it would be nearly impossible to carry the stores from the ship to the land, and wholly impossible to get the ponies and motor sledges across.

So the *Terra Nova* sailed on, and five miles east

of Cape Crozier came to the Barrier. This was a great sheet of ice more than four hundred miles wide, and of much greater length, which lay to the west of Victoria Land. In height, the Barrier was not more than sixty feet.

Scott now determined to winter at a point which had been known to the crew of the *Discovery* as the Skuary, but which was renamed by Scott Cape Evans, in honour of E. Evans, the second in command.

When about a mile from the Skuary, the ship struck on hard ice. Anchors were at once let down, and Scott, E. Evans, and Wilson set out across the ice to inspect the Cape where they hoped to winter.

The position pleased them, for here they could not easily be cut off from the Barrier. There was, too, a beach protected by several small hills, on which their hut could be built. Scott decided to begin at once to unload the ship.

Two motor sledges were first hauled on to the ice, which formed a safe and useful wharf. So well had they been protected by tarpaulin covers that when these were stripped off, the motors were as bright as though no heavy seas had washed over them.

Most of the ponies were coaxed by Oates into the horse-box, but some had to be lifted in by the sailors. After their cramped position in the stalls, they enjoyed being able to stretch themselves on the floe and were soon frisking about, the misery they had endured forgotten.

Meanwhile, Meares had got his dog teams out, and harnessed to the sledges, they were already at work carrying stores from the ship to the Cape. The dogs would have given no trouble had not the penguins been curious about the strange creatures that had invaded their haunts. They stepped fearlessly toward the dogs; they poked their heads forward in their desire to examine these unknown objects.

This was more than the dogs could stand, and they made a dash to reach the birds, but were held back by their harness. Unalarmed, the birds waddled nearer still, making an angry noise and with their ruffles standing up. One rash bird ventured too close, and in a moment a dog's paw had descended and the foolish penguin was seen no more. In spite of the loss of a comrade or two, the birds refused to be driven away and went on with their study of the new arrivals.

The next morning all hands were at work by six o'clock, building the hut which was to be their home.

While the men were at work, Scott saw a strange sight. In front of the ship, close to an ice floe, were six or seven whales, called killer whales. After diving again and again, they appeared astern of the ship, near the spot where the two Esquimaux dogs chanced to be tethered.

Ponting, one of the scientific staff, was on shore with his camera, and he ran to the edge of the floe to take a photograph of the whales. But they had dived again and were for the moment out of sight. As Ponting waited for them to appear, the floe on which he and the dogs stood suddenly broke into pieces. Ponting managed to reach a place of safety, while the dogs were left each on a separate piece of ice and surrounded by water.

This is what had happened: the whales had struck the ice with their backs with such force that the floe had been splintered into fragments. These fragments swayed dangerously as the whales rose to the surface and thrust their huge heads through the cracks they had made. Scott said it was plain that they were looking to see what had become of the man and the dogs. Soon afterwards, the whales disappeared, and the dogs, who were now shivering with fear, were rescued from the dangerous ice island on which they had been stranded.

It was no new thing for killer whales to skirt the edge of floes, but the strength they had shown in breaking ice which was 2½ feet thick surprised everyone, while the wise way in which they seemed

OFF STARTED THE PONY AT A GALLOP

to have planned their attack amazed the men even more.

During the week spent in unloading the ship and while the hut was being built, the ponies and dogs were not always easy to manage. The ponies were restive on the ice, and each seemed to fear that if he stopped, the sledge which he drew would run him down.

One day a pony stood on the ice beside the ship while the sledge to which he was harnessed was being loaded. Suddenly, off started the pony at a gallop, never stopping until he reached the camp, where his load tumbled off.

Oates had charge of the ponies and was devoted to them. Scott was quick to note his care for the animals, and wrote, "Oates is splendid with them. I do not know what we should do without him."

Sometimes the dogs were seized with a spirit of adventure. Once a team ran away, and as it started, one of the dogs was knocked down. The beast tried in vain to struggle to his feet and was dragged along for about half a mile. But the escapade seemed to do him no harm.

A more serious accident nearly happened, this time to one of the men.

Ponting had gone off alone on a small sledge with his camera. As he tramped along, harnessed to the sledge, he suddenly felt that the ice beneath his feet was giving way. No one was within reach; no one could hear if he shouted for help. He hurried on, the ice cracking and crumbling at each step, the sledge dragging through water. But a little farther on he reached a firm piece of ice and knew that he was safe.

The weather had begun to trouble the men. Some suffered from snow blindness; others had their faces and their feet cut or blistered by the wind.

"Such things are part of the business," wrote Scott.

CHAPTER V

THE JOURNEY TO ONE TON CAMP

CAPE EVANS is a spur of Mount Erebus. Here, on a stretch of black sand, sheltered at the back by a small hill, the site for the hut was chosen.

In front of the camp stretched the sea, dotted here and there with floating ice floes, while far in the distance, but standing out clearly, were the Western Mountains.

A hut was scarcely the right word for the building at which the men were working with such goodwill. It was a house large enough to be comfortable for those who were to winter in it.

So well did the men work that the hut could have been inhabited eight days after the ship had been unloaded. But the carpenter wished to finish the inside of the house before the men settled down in their winter quarters.

At the back of the camp stood hard snowdrift, and two or three men were sent to clear it away.

They soon reached solid ice, so they determined to cut out a cave which could be used as a larder.

Sunday, the 15th January, no work was done, but in the morning the officers and men from the ship joined those at camp, and service was held in the open air.

In the afternoon, Scott and Meares set off with a sledge drawn by nine dogs to Hut Point, close to Discovery Hut. To their disappointment, they found the hut full of snow, and so could not spend the night in it as they had hoped to do.

The door had been blown in by the force of the wind, and when a party led by Shackleton had reached it some time before, they had had to go in by the window. Unfortunately, the window had been left open, and the snow which had filled the hut was now frozen hard.

Scott and Meares returned to the camp next day, and on the 17th January the land party settled into their new quarters at Cape Evans.

The cook, who was named Clissold, proved a skilful one, making dishes of seal, penguin, and skua in such tempting forms that everyone enjoyed mealtime and ate well.

"I have never met these articles of food in such pleasing guise," wrote Scott. "This point is of the

DISCOVERY HUT.

greatest practical importance, as it means the certainty of good health for any number of years."

Plans now began to be made for a depôt journey. Depôts or huts were to be built at certain points on the road, and food and fodder left at each to be used on the return journey.

But before the depôt party started, Scott went on board the *Terra Nova*, which was now soon to return to New Zealand. The men were called together on deck, and Scott thanked them all for the ungrudging way they had worked during the voyage.

"They have behaved like bricks," he wrote of them in his journal, "and a finer lot of fellows never sailed in a ship. It was good to get their hearty send-off."

Twelve men were chosen for the depôt journey. With them they took eight ponies and twenty-six dogs. When they reached their second camp, which was on the Barrier and which was named Safety Camp, Atkinson had to be left behind in charge of Crean. His foot had had to be lanced, and it was impossible for him to march with the others. Both Atkinson and Crean were bitterly disappointed.

Those who went on with Scott were E. Evans, Forde, Keohane, Meares, Wilson, Bowers, Oates, Cherry-Garrard. Gran, Meares and Wilson were in charge of the dog-teams.

The ponies found the soft snow so difficult that

a pair of snow-shoes were fitted on one of them, named Weary Willie. This made him step out almost as though he was walking on hard ground. But only one pair had been brought away from Cape Evans, so Meares and Wilson set out for the camp, which was now twenty miles away, to get others. The next day they came back without the shoes, for they had found a big expanse of water between them and the Cape, which made it impossible to reach the camp.

On the 2nd February the party set out with food for five weeks. They expected to spend about twelve days on the outward march before returning to Safety Camp, which was to be the big home depôt station.

The snow was so soft that Scott decided to march during the night and early morning. Even then there were snow patches over which the ponies drew their loads with difficulty.

When the poor creatures felt themselves sinking, they made desperate struggles to escape, and if the patch was small they succeeded. Sometimes when the patch was larger they plunged about, dragging the sledge forward by sudden jerks, until they grew exhausted and were half covered in the snow. "The quiet lazy ponies have a much better time than the eager ones when such troubles arise," wrote Scott.

At their fifth camp, called Corner Camp, the party

was overtaken by a blizzard. But when the men got into their sleeping-bags, they were comfortable, and even warm, and could forget that a storm was raging outside the tent.

The next day the storm was fiercer than ever, and it was not easy to shield the ponies from the blizzard, but the dogs curled themselves up in holes in the snow and came out at mealtimes in good condition.

Although the storm did not last long, the ponies had grown thinner before it was over, and when the party set out once more, one of the animals had to have his load made smaller. Even then he gave in before the day's march was over.

Soon after this, three of the ponies grew so weak that Scott determined to send them back with E. Evans, Forde, and Keohane. The five others he hoped would be able to go on for a few days longer.

But again a blizzard delayed the travellers, and when it was over, the surface was so bad that the ponies sank again and again in snowdrifts.

Weary Willie dropped behind, then fell, and before Meares could prevent it, his dog-team was attacking the unfortunate beast. He was badly beaten, although he tried to defend himself, before Meares and Gran could drive off the dogs. They covered him with sacking, gave him a hot meal, and when the next camp was reached, a large snow wall was built to protect Weary Willie from the cold.

A day or two later, three of the five ponies were so weak that Scott made up his mind to go no farther. So the men made their fifteenth camp and built a depôt in which they stored provisions. The spot was marked with a flagstaff on which was hung a black flag, which would be seen clearly against the great stretch of snow.

Biscuit boxes too, both full and empty, were piled up one on the top of the other and tied to sledges which had been placed upright in the snow. These would act as reflectors, and the depôt would be seen many miles away.

The cold had tried the men as well as the animals. Oates' nose was on the verge of being frost-bitten, while Meares' toes suffered greatly from cold.

CHAPTER VI

THE ACCIDENT TO THE DOG-TEAM

ONLY twelve miles to Safety Camp! The travellers had marched back so far when an accident befell the dog-team.

The night march began as usual about 10 p.m., and soon it grew difficult to see the surface.

As the men ran along with their teams, Wilson suddenly shouted, "Hold on to the sledge!" A few moments later the team driven by Scott and Meares disappeared into a crevasse, each pair of dogs struggling hard to get a foothold as they fell. Osman, the leader, alone succeeded.

The sledge had stopped on the edge of the crevasse. Had the load it carried been the slightest degree heavier, it would almost certainly have fallen into the chasm, carrying the drivers with it.

When Scott and Meares had pulled the sledge aside, they looked down, and there were all the dogs, save two, suspended over the crevasse by their harness. They were howling and terribly frightened.

Two had been shaken out of their trappings and had dropped on to a snow-bridge farther down the abyss.

Osman, although he had not fallen over, was lying with the leading rope of the sledge entangled round his throat so that he was nearly choked. The first task, which was no easy one, was to loosen the rope and set Osman free from his harness.

When this was done, the Alpine rope was fastened to the sledge, and the men tried to haul the terrified dogs to the surface. Before they could succeed, they were forced to run the sledge across the crevasse. Standing on it, they could handle the rope with more ease.

At length, all were rescued save the two dogs that had fallen on to the snow-bridge, about sixty-five feet below. To the distress of the others, Scott decided that he would go to the help of the poor animals. He was lowered with care and succeeded in tying the animals to the rope, so that both were drawn safely to the surface.

Before Scott himself could be hauled up, the men were forced to rush to separate the dogs, for those who had been rescued had attacked the team harnessed to the first sledge and a furious fight had begun.

They were soon separated, and the men hastened

THE MEN HASTENED BACK TO RELEASE SCOTT FROM HIS PERILOUS POSITION.

back to release Scott from his perilous position. It had taken nearly two hours to rescue all the animals, and Scott now resolved to camp that they might rest and have food after their exertions. Not only their efforts, but the shock had told upon them all, for they knew they had had a narrow escape — if not from death, at least from serious injury.

Safety Camp was reached without farther disaster, but the dogs were thinner than when they set out, while their appetites were enormous.

This short journey showed Scott that the dogs' rations would need to be increased on the next expedition. He was convinced, too, that the Russian custom of sitting on the sledge must be given up, and that the men must learn to run along by the side of their dog-teams.

E. Evans and his companions awaited Scott at

Safety Camp. On their way back, they had encountered a blizzard, from which one pony had suffered so severely that he died. Another pony, named Blossom, had gone on ten miles and then begun to flag. A few yards farther, he had stopped, his legs apart, his head drooping to the ground. He had been fed, allowed to rest, covered with rugs, but he too had died. The third pony, James Pigg, was well and able to do light work.

It was now that Scott received the letter which told him that Amundsen, the Norwegian explorer, was in the Bay of Whales. He was from this point sixty miles nearer the Pole than Scott, and he would be able to set out earlier in the year because he had no ponies with him.

Scott had dreamed of the honour he would bring to his country by being the first to plant a flag at the South Pole. He now feared that Amundsen might outstrip him. Yet he determined to act as though he had not heard of the rival on the field, and he still hoped his dream might be fulfilled.

On the 5th March the party reached Discovery Hut, out of which the snow had been cleared. It was plain that they would have to stay there for some time, as where ice had been, water now cut them off from Cape Evans.

So the men set to work to make the hut as comfortable as possible. They had some trouble with the stove, which, when filled with blubber, began to smoke, and soon each one in the camp was almost too begrimed to recognize the other. Their clothes, too, smelt of oil and were covered with soot.

They were well off for provisions, for not only necessary food had been stored in the hut, but chocolates, raisins, sardines, jams, and other luxuries as well.

No sooner had they settled down in their new home than a blizzard began to rage, and day after day it showed no sign of abating. The dogs suffered from want of exercise, and at last five or six were allowed to run loose. But the stronger ones had to be kept chained, as they were always ready to attack the weaker ones.

One of the dogs that had been rescued from the crevasse had been hurt by its fall, and it died at Hut Point, while three were ill.

Osman did not seem to feel the weather, but the ice got into the coats of the others and froze their hind legs. "Bit by bit I am losing all faith in the dogs," wrote Scott. "I'm afraid they will never go the pace we look for."

CHAPTER VII

THE TRAVELLERS REACH CAPE EVANS

SCOTT had hoped to be back at Cape Evans by the beginning of April, but the storms were so persistent that it was about the middle of the month before he could leave Hut Point. Wilson stayed behind with six of the men.

The others on their homeward journey encamped one night on sea ice. Before morning a blizzard was raging, and it seemed as though the ice on which the camp was pitched might be driven out to sea. As the wind blew more fiercely, Scott grew anxious and went out with Bowers to look for a safer spot for the tent. They found a small portion of ice, sheltered by high cliffs, to which the camp was moved. The cold was so intense that the men could only work slowly, and two hours passed before their task was done. But at last they could lie down, knowing that they would not be swept away to sea. As the wind whistled across the top of the cliffs, Scott must have wondered if it would be possible to march in the morning. It was necessary to reach Cape Evans without delay, for in the camp there was food for only one more meal. In spite of the storm, the party reached Cape Evans the following day. Scott had often, in his absence, feared lest a blizzard of unusual violence should have swept away the hut and stables at the winter station, so it was with great relief that as he turned the last corner he saw that all was standing safe as when he left.

No sooner was the return of the travellers known than everyone in the camp rushed to greet them and to hear their adventures.

In a very short time, too, Scott had been told all that had happened during his absence and had been taken to see the improvements that had been made in the camp.

Everything he saw and heard gave him great pleasure, his only disappointment being that one pony and one dog had died.

Four days after his return, Scott went back with some of the men to Hut Point. Blizzards had kept Wilson indoors and the supply of blubber was almost at an end. But soon after Scott's arrival, three seals were captured.

When Scott returned to Cape Evans, he took with him Wilson, Atkinson, Crean, Bowers, Oates,

Cherry-Garrard, and Hooper, while Meares was left behind with Demetri, Lashly, Keohane, Nelson, Day, and Forde.

A plentiful meal of rice and figs, with a bucketful of cocoa, awaited the travellers at the camp.

CHAPTER VIII

THE WINTER SEASON

THE long dark days of winter were now at hand. For several months there would be no sunlight in this southern land. The 23rd April was the last day on which those at the home station saw the sun.

During the winter, everyone was busy with his own particular piece of work. The scientific men made experiments and carried out observations. Oates attended to the ponies. "His whole heart is in his ponies," Scott wrote in his journal. Petty Officer, or as we will call him, P. O. Evans, and Crean spent their time mending sleeping-bags and covering boots. Clissold still surprised everyone with new dishes for dinner.

Lectures, too, were given, the first one being by Wilson on "Antarctic Flying Birds." But the one which roused the greatest interest was that given by Scott himself. His subject was a sketch of his plans for reaching the Pole. In his journal he wrote, "It is going to be a tough job; that is better realized the more one dives into it."

The men played football during these winter months, when there was enough light. It was almost the only exercise they had out of doors.

Food was of importance and interest to Scott because on it depended the health of his men. Here is a day's menu, which, with a few alterations, was the usual fare.

For breakfast: porridge and two small fish each, bread and butter and marmalade. For lunch: bread and butter and cheese, cake. While for dinner there was seal soup, seal steak and kidney pie, and fruit jelly.

On Sundays a service was held in the hut, which ended with "their own special prayer." After service, the men usually went out with the ponies.

Scott's birthday on the 6th June broke the monotony of the days. Clissold made a big cake for lunch to celebrate the event. It was adorned with flags and designs in chocolate, while photographs of the hero completed its decoration.

"It is my birthday," wrote Scott, "a fact I might easily have forgotten, but my kind people did not."

The 22nd June was midwinter in these regions, and the day was kept as we keep Christmas Day at home.

I need not tell you of the wonderful dinner Clissold prepared, for you know his skill as a cook, but there certainly was a flaming plum pudding on the table, and when dinner was over, everyone drank "Success to the Expedition."

But the chief event of the evening was a Christmas tree, which Bowers carried in, ablaze with candles and sparkling with crackers. On the tree there was a present for each. The tree was not a fir tree but one made out of a piece of stick, covered with coloured papers.

While the merriment was at its height, Scott, with one or two others, slipped out of the hut to watch the eastern sky, which was lit up by a wonderful light more beautiful than Scott had ever seen. "It is impossible," he wrote, "to witness such a phenomenon without a sense of awe. There is no glittering splendour to dazzle the eye; rather the appeal is to the imagination by the suggestion of something wholly spiritual, something instinct with a fluttering ethereal life."

Is there a note of foreboding in the words with which he closed his journal on the "High Festival of Midwinter"? "After all," he wrote, "we celebrated the birth of a season which for weal or woe must be numbered amongst the greatest in our lives."

CHAPTER IX

THE WANDERER

AGAIN and again Scott wrote about the friendship and goodwill that never failed in the camp during those dark, trying months. "There is no friction at all," we read. "There are no strained relations in the hut. It is a triumph to have collected such men."

During the month of June, Wilson, Bowers, and Cherry-Garrard set out on an expedition to Cape Crozier, each dragging a heavy load of 250 lbs. They wished to reach a rookery of penguins, in which Wilson was specially interested.

Of the blizzards they encountered, of the terrible struggle they had to reach the Cape, I may not stop to tell. But after five weeks they were back at Cape Evans, showing plainly in their faces what they had undergone. Each had lost in weight — Wilson, 3½ lbs.; Bowers, 2½ lbs.; and Cherry-Garrard, 1 lb.

While they were away, except for one terrible gale, nothing disturbed the routine of the camp, until one day at dinner-time it was found that Atkinson was not in the camp. He had gone out with Gran,

SCOTT, WITH ONE OR TWO OTHERS, SLIPPED OUT OF
THE TENT TO WATCH THE EASTERN SKY.

but after a time they had separated and Gran had returned long ago.

As snow was falling, Scott sent several men out to shout and swing lanterns up and down, while a blaze of paraffin was lit on a hill, in the hope that it might attract the attention of the wanderer and guide him toward the camp.

Meanwhile, the moon began to shine, and this was more likely to lead Atkinson home than any of the other lights. But when a search party returned about 9:30 without him, it seemed that an accident must have befallen the unfortunate man.

Search parties were now sent out in all directions, Scott and Clissold alone waiting in the camp. Not until 11:45 did the lost man appear with Meares and Debenham. The frost had bitten his hand badly; his face, too, had suffered, although not so severely.

He was asked what had happened but seemed unable to tell, for he was bewildered, as often happens to those who have been lost in a blizzard.

Scott wrote that in such storms it was not only circulation of the limbs that had to be looked after, but that it was necessary "to fight a sluggishness of brain and an absence of reasoning power," which was often the cause of disaster.

All that Atkinson could tell was that he had lost his way in the blizzard and that it was the appearance of the moon that had helped him to turn in the direction of the camp.

He had seen the paraffin blaze on the hill and said that he had called to someone who seemed quite close to him but had received no answer.

"This is the story of a half-thawed brain," wrote Scott.

But Atkinson's strange condition made everyone realize, as he had not done before, the danger of being lost in a blizzard.

Another event that disturbed the camp was the illness of Bones, one of the best ponies. He was looked after with great care, for it would be a serious matter to lose another pony. But he seemed to grow worse and worse. In the end, however, Bones repaid the patience and care spent upon him, for he recovered. China also had a slight attack, but he was better in half an hour.

The dark days and bad weather were beginning to try the health and spirits of both men and beasts. Scott longed for the light of the sun once more, for that, he wrote, "should cure all ailments, physical and mental."

CHAPTER X

THE RETURN OF THE SUN

TOWARD the end of August, light began to increase. The ponies showed their pleasure by escaping from their drivers when they could, galloping off, frisking their tails, and kicking up their heels. The dogs, too, grew livelier now that they could have more exercise.

One day, Scott climbed to the top of a hill with Ponting, and to their delight, they found themselves bathed in sunshine. By the beginning of October, meals were eaten in daylight, and even the night was no longer dark.

Preparations were now being made for the journey to the South Pole. The eleven men chosen by Scott to go with him on the Southern journey were Wilson, Oates, P. O. Evans, who went with Scott himself on the first sledge; E. Evans, Atkinson, Wright, Lashly, who were with the second sledge, while with the third went Bowers, Cherry-Garrard, Crean, and Keohane.

Of these eleven men Scott wrote: "There does

SOMETIMES ONE OF HIS FORELEGS HAD TO BE TIED.

not seem to be a single weak spot in the eleven good men and true who are chosen for the Southern advance." Each had had experience of sledge travelling. Each, too, was bound to the other in a strong bond of comradeship.

Two others, Day and Hooper, went with the motor sledge for three weeks and then turned homewards, while Meares and Demetri, with the dog-teams, went as far as the Low Glacier Depôt, returning on the 11th of December. During these weeks, the ponies again caused great anxiety. Scott knew that none could be spared, and while Day was sure the motors would do wonders, Scott did not think he should count upon them.

Jehu, one of the ponies, proved too weak to pull his load. Christopher could never be harnessed to his sledge without great trouble. Sometimes one of his forelegs had to be tied before it could be done. He was left to start on three legs, and when at length the fourth was unbound, he ran quietly. At times he was so restive that he had to be thrown on the ground, and even when he was on his knees, it was not safe to venture too near for fear he should kick with his hind legs.

Victor, Snippets, Nobby, Bones, and little Michael were in good condition, while Chinaman and James

Pigg were fit for work, though not able to do so much as the others.

The trouble with the ponies was forgotten for a time in anxiety about Clissold. He slipped from a berg and, as he fell, struck his head and back and was carried to camp unconscious. The injury was not serious, but it made it impossible for him to go with the motor party as Scott had meant him to do. Hooper was chosen in his stead.

A few days after Clissold's accident, Deek, one of the strongest dogs, died after a night's illness. But in spite of trouble and disappointment, the preparations for the journey went on steadily. The motor sledges were tested for several days, and at length, on the 31st of October, Atkinson and Keohane set off, the rest of the party being ready to start the following day.

CHAPTER XI

THE JOURNEY

ON the 1st of November, the Southern party left Cape Evans and the next day reached Hut Point.

The ponies did well, Snatcher with P. O. Evans racing ahead of the others and reaching Hut Point in four hours. He seemed as fresh when he arrived as when he started. Christopher spent a great deal of energy kicking as he went along, but he showed no trace of tiredness when he reached the camp.

Scott arranged that the following day the slow ponies should start first, then those that went at a moderate pace, and last of all the ones that raced. Snatcher, he thought, would reach — if not pass — the leading ponies although he started last. It was also arranged to march at night.

As the men left their second camp, they found a note left by Day to tell that the motors were running well. When they had marched four miles, they found another note saying that a cylinder had broken. Half a mile farther, they found a deserted motor, for E. Evans and Day had decided to go on with one sledge rather than spend time in repairing the other. "So the dream of great help from the machines is at an end," wrote Scott, for he expected each hour to find that the other motor had also broken down.

At Corner Camp, which was the third camp, another note awaited them. E. Evans reported that the motor was now running only seven miles a day. In the distance, a black object could be seen, and this, as Scott feared, proved to be the second motor, which the men had left behind.

When the travellers reached their fourth camp, a blizzard was blowing, and the tents were soon half covered with drifting snow. Inside the tent the men were comfortable and even warm, but the ponies suffered from the cold, although walls of snow were built to protect them from the wind.

After the blizzard was over, the men were cheered by a few days of sunshine. They marched on, finding without difficulty the cairns which had been built the year before on the journey to One Ton Camp. These, Scott hoped, would help them to keep to the track on the homeward journey.

The warm weather soon passed, and for three or four days afterward, Scott describes the marches as "uniformly horrid."

Meanwhile, the ponies were doing well, although Atkinson thought that Chinaman would only be able to march a mile or two more. Jehu had surprised everyone by the amount he could do.

But the condition of the ponies never ceased to trouble Scott. "If they pull through well, all the thanks will be due to Oates," he wrote in his journal.

It was seldom that a note of apprehension stole into Scott's diary. His outlook was always brave and nearly always hopeful. But the weather was unusually bad for the time of year, and he seemed to fear what it might forebode. The camp, which was usually full of cheer, grew silent under the strain of these days.

On the 15th November, One Ton Camp was reached, and here, for the sake of the ponies, Scott rested for a day.

At the camp, they found a note from E. Evans, who had left about seven days earlier, carrying from the depôt four boxes of biscuits. "I only hope he has built lots of cairns," wrote Scott. It had been misty for four days, and the great snow plain would have seemed a trackless waste without these landmarks.

To avoid snow blindness, most of the men were now wearing green-tinted goggles.

CHAPTER XII

SHAMBLES CAMP

ON the 21st November, the travellers reached the motor party. The men were well, but thin, Day being "almost gaunt." They had been very hungry, for the rations that were enough for men who were leading ponies were "not enough for those who were hauling heavy loads."

On the summit, Scott knew they would be hungrier still, but this he had foreseen, and the rations were arranged to satisfy larger appetites.

Jehu had now done nearly all the work he was able to do. He seemed scarcely able to pull a load at all, and the poor animal was shot.

Meares needed food for his dogs and was glad to have horse flesh. He could make it last for four meals, and if another pony gave in, he knew there would be enough to take the dogs to the Glacier.

Four days after Scott reached them, Day and Hooper turned homewards, while the others marched forward with the wearied beasts. At each new depôt, the ponies' loads were made lighter.

Soon after leaving the Middle Barrier Depôt, snow began to fall, and the wind rose, driving it straight into the faces of the travellers.

In spite of this, they marched as far as usual before they stopped to camp. It was no easy task to pitch the tents, as the snow was still falling and drifting. Before the party left the snowed-up camp, Chinaman was shot.

When at length the storm was over, the men set out gladly. It was good to be marching again towards the goal. They found the surface easy, but the ponies were constantly sinking in drifts up to their knees.

On the 1st of December, Christopher was shot, and the Southern Barrier Depôt was built. As they left the depôt, snow was again falling, and the ponies struggled on, plunging and sinking in the drifts.

From a diary telling of Shackleton's journey, we know that until the middle of December, he had had good weather. About the beginning of the month, Scott wrote: "With us, a fine day has been the exception so far." But he had not cut down the regular day's march in spite of the difficulties he had met.

At their thirtieth camp, the travellers were delayed for four days, so fierce a storm was raging. Scott was growing anxious in case they encountered the same terrible weather on the Glacier, where, even in fine weather, marching would be difficult. It was at this camp that the snowfall was the heaviest Scott had ever known.

"What on earth does such weather mean at this time of year? No foresight could have prepared us for this state of affairs," he wrote.

Keohane refused to be depressed while the blizzard raged. He attempted to write a rhyme on the storm. It was not a very good rhyme, but it amused the others. You will like to read it:

"The snow is all melting and everything afloat,
If this goes on much longer, we shall have to turn
The tent upside down and use it as a boat."

Still, the storm raged, and Scott wrote that they had camped in the "Slough of Despond."

Higher and higher rose the snow until the pony walls were covered and the tents were no longer to be seen. There was little merriment now in the camp, and despair all but took possession of the leader of the party. But he fought gallantly against the feeling of hopelessness that was getting him in its grip.

The delay made big demands upon the food supply, and the men were now forced to begin the rations which should have been untouched until they reached the Glacier Depôt.

When at length they were able to get off, the soft snow made marching almost impossible for the ponies. P. O. Evans put the only pair of pony snow-shoes they possessed on Snatcher. This helped him to go on more easily, and the others followed him well. But when the camp was pitched, the ponies were utterly exhausted, and it was necessary to put them out of misery. They were all killed, and the camp was given the gruesome name of Shambles Camp.

Although the future was gloomy, the men's spirits were good, and Scott wrote at this, the thirty-first camp: "Everyone is cheerful tonight, and jokes are flying freely around."

CHAPTER XIII

THE SUMMIT

THE Southern party had now parted with Meares and Demetri, as well as Day and Hooper.

On the 10th December, those going onward set out in three divisions, each division hauling a sledge which had to plough its way through the snow. After a day's march, they built the Lower Glacier Depôt, where they left provisions and whatever they could do without, so that they might march more easily.

One day, the surface was so bad that the men could only cover four miles. They had hoped, as they climbed higher, that it would be better and the weather less changeable, but in this, they were disappointed.

"We can but toil on, it is woefully disheartening," wrote Scott about this time.

As they ascended, the sun was often so hot that the travellers flung off some of their garments, but when they stopped marching, they felt the cold severely, for their skins were burnt and sensitive.

Often, too, they suffered from thirst, and as they went along, sucked pieces of ice.

It was soon necessary to arrange which of the men should be the next to return. "I dreaded this necessity of choosing; nothing could be more heart-rending," wrote Scott.

The only way was to keep those whom he believed would be best able to endure the hardships that they would certainly have to face. So Atkinson, Wright, Cherry-Garrard, and Keohane were sent back, while Scott went on with Wilson, Oates, and P. O. Evans in the first sledge. E. Evans, Bowers, Crean, and Lashly followed in the second.

On the 21st December, the summit was reached, and in spite of delays, the travellers were now only one day's food in advance. "We ought to get through," is Scott's comment in his journal. Each day, as the loads grew lighter, it was easier to march, and they were able to do nine hours instead of seven.

Once, the men found themselves among narrow crevasses over which snow had hardened, so that they were unseen. Each of the travellers fell through the crust of one or another of these pitfalls. No one was hurt seriously, but time was lost in scrambling out of the hole. In spite of this, they marched fifteen miles in about eight and a half hours, while they mounted about 800 feet. It was a day of good omen, and Scott wrote: "I am feeling very cheerful about everything tonight. To me, for the first time, our goal seems really in sight."

On Christmas Eve, the thought of Christmas fare on the morrow encouraged everyone.

Four courses were provided, and the supplies were so plentiful that Scott and Wilson did not finish their share of plum pudding. The good meal made them warm, and they slept sooner and better than usual.

The early days of the New Year 1912 brought disappointment to three of the travellers. Scott decided that E. Evans, Lashly, and Crean should return. It was a great blow to the men. Crean shed tears when he said goodbye to his leader and his companions, while Lashly did not hide his grief. E. Evans felt it keenly, but Scott wrote, "He has taken it well and behaved like a man."

Only five of the party were now left — Scott, Wilson, Oates, Bowers, and P. O. Evans. On and on they marched, over monotonous stretches of snow, each day much like the other. They felt that now they were nearing their goal, that now they might build castles in the air. They dreamed that they would reach the South Pole before the Norwegians.

But the surface was bad, and their progress was slow. A blizzard delayed them for a day, but while

Scott decided that E. Evans, Lashly and Crean should return.

the snow was still drifting, they set out, and after marching six and a half miles, they found themselves beyond the farthest spot that Shackleton had reached. Their path would now be over ground untrodden before by Englishmen.

On the 10th of January, they built a depôt and then went forward with food for eighteen days. The sunshine on the snow made the glare almost unendurable. To haul the sledges was almost beyond the men's strength. Scott wrote that when the sun was out, it was "agonizing work to pull." To march six miles was a supreme effort.

Only seventy-four miles from their goal! But unless the weather and the surface improved, it was doubtful if it could be done in the time that Scott had expected.

Hauling with all their might at the sledges, which were now really light, the men yet made little progress. "O for a few fine days," wrote Scott on the 14th of January. The next day the last depôt was built.

As the travellers drew nearer to the Pole, they often thought of the Norwegians. Would they have reached the goal? Would their flag be planted already at the South Pole?

One day, Bowers saw in the distance what he hoped was a cairn, what he feared was something else. The travellers hastened on to find their fears realized, their castles in the air thrown roughly to the ground. For there, near a deserted camp, tied to a sledge-bearer, hung a black flag.

Scott's disappointment was keen, but in the midst of his own grief, he wrote, "I am very sorry for my loyal companions." He determined to hasten on to the Pole and then start on the homeward journey as quickly as possible.

But the zest had been taken out of the expedition, and cold feet and cold hands seemed harder to bear now that their hopes had been dashed. There was little sleep for any of the explorers after the Norwegian flag had been seen.

"This is an awful place," wrote Scott, "and terrible enough for us to have laboured to it, without the reward of priority. Well, it is something to have got here, and the wind may be our friend tomorrow."

The next day they came to a tent in which they found the names of five Norwegians: heading the list stood that of Roald Amundsen.

About half a mile from the Pole, the disheartened men set up their camp, calling it Pole Camp. Here they built a cairn and put on it the "poor slighted Union Jack."

A little distance from their camp, they found the under-runner of a sledge which the Norwegians had planted on what they thought must be the nearest spot to the Pole.

The Pole was about 9,500 feet in height. This surprised the travellers, for at one part of their journey, they had reached 10,500 feet. They placed the Union Jack on the exact spot of the South Pole as nearly as they could judge, and then they prepared for the homeward journey.

"Well, we have turned our back now on the goal of our ambition," wrote Scott, "and must face our 800 miles of solid dragging — and good-bye to most of our day-dreams."

CHAPTER XIV

THE STRUGGLE

ALMOST from the beginning of the return journey, misfortune began to dog the steps of the travellers, although at first the track was plain and the cairns were seen without difficulty.

P. O. Evans was suffering from frostbitten nose and fingers, Oates from cold feet, and Wilson from snow blindness. Ski boots, too, looked as if they would be worn out before the end of the journey, which would be a serious matter.

The weather was so bad that after five days the men found themselves in the midst of a second blizzard. The outlook was gloomy, and Scott wrote, "Is the weather breaking up? If so, God help us with the tremendous summit journey and scant food."

Every delay now caused anxiety. Sometimes the track was covered with snowdrifts and could not be found. Then, after some miles, the travellers were gladdened by seeing it again quite clearly. But hours were often lost searching for the right direction.

Along the old tracks, they found one day Oates'

THEY PANTED THE UNION JACK ON THE EXACT SPOT AS NEARLY AS THEY COULD

JUDGE

pipe, Bowers' fur mitts, and Evans' night boots. These had been dropped on the outward march.

Day by day, the men grew more hungry, and their rations were far from satisfying, nor was there any hope of increasing them until they came to the first pony food depôt.

By the end of January, the travellers reached Three Degree Depôt, but Wilson had strained a tendon in his leg, and P. O. Evans' hands were so bad that he lost two fingernails. The strain of all they had undergone showed more plainly in Evans than in the others.

Scott was the healthiest of them all when, a few days later, he slipped on a steep slope and hurt his shoulder, which by night was "horribly sore."

"Three out of five injured," he wrote sadly. "We shall be lucky if we get through without serious injury."

Twice within the next few days, Evans fell into a crevasse, Scott falling with him the first time. Such shocks were good for neither, but told seriously on Evans, who after these falls seemed to grow rapidly worse. He was suffering from slight concussion and was dull and heavy.

The travellers had secured a supply of food at the last depôt, but in spite of good meals, their hunger seemed to increase.

In a short time, food was again scarce, while the weather was now good, now bad. No day passed without many hours of gloom and foreboding. And each time Scott mentioned Evans in his journal, it was in a more hopeless way. On the 6th of February, the record was that he seemed nearly played out.

After hardships greater than I have been able to tell, the men reached the Upper Glacier Depôt, and the summit journey was over. Here they found a note left by E. Evans to say he had passed the depôt safely.

Scott hoped that now the worst was over, but after marching for four days, the men lost the tracks and found themselves among more dangerous ice than Scott had ever seen. Every moment they kept falling into crevasses, and it seemed as though they would never reach the right way.

Hour after hour, they struggled on, going now to the right, now to the left. It was only after about twelve hours that they found themselves back on the old tracks. But they had now very little food, and they were still some miles from the next depôt.

They set out early the next morning so as to be sure of reaching the depôt that night. But once again, they went in the wrong direction, and were soon forced to camp in a maze of crevasses. After a scanty supper, there was food left for only one more meal. "Pray God we have fine weather," Scott wrote in his journal that night.

The men were too tired not to sleep, though Scott went out of the tent more than once to study the sky. It was clouding over, and before morning, snow began to fall. When the usual time to march came, snow was lying thick around the camp, and there was nothing the men could do but stay in their sleeping bags.

About nine o'clock, they had tea and one biscuit each, and then set out once more to look for the track. Broken ice made the march terribly hard, but they were desperate and struggled on. At last, to the relief of each, the lost track was seen stretching before them.

On they went, cheered by a shout from Evans, who pointed ahead to an object which he thought was the depôt. It was only a shadow on the ice. But the depôt was not really far away, and Wilson soon caught sight of the flag that marked its position.

To have food safe for three and a half days was a great relief. But the strain of the last hours had been tremendous, and Scott wrote, "Yesterday was the worst experience of the trip and gave a horrid feeling of insecurity."

Evans was now too weak to help with the camp. His foot was blistered, and the others had to march

SCOTT WENT OUT OF THE TENT MORE THAN ONCE TO STUDY THE SKY.

slowly or they would have left him behind. He was eager for more food than he could have, for the next depôt was thirty miles away, and Scott did not dare to give full rations.

The sick man added greatly to the difficulty of each day's march. He had been one of the most capable and sturdy of the party, but he was now quite unlike himself. Twice in one day, he stopped the march on some paltry pretext, as it seemed. In reality, he was too ill to keep up with the others.

On the 17th of February, the sick man set out with the others, seeming a little better after a night's rest. But before long, his ski shoes troubled him, and he dropped behind. Had the others not waited, he would scarcely have reached them again.

About half an hour later, he stopped again, saying he must fasten his ski shoes and asking Bowers to lend him string. Scott warned him not to linger far behind. The others then marched on, finding it hard work to pull over the soft snow.

By and by, Scott camped for lunch, expecting Evans to arrive before it was finished. But the sick man did not come, and when his comrades looked back, they saw him still in the distance. So, they put on their ski shoes and went back to meet him.

Scott reached him first and found him in a desperate plight. He was kneeling on the snow, his frostbitten hands uncovered, his eyes wild and strange. When he was asked what had happened, he said he thought he had fainted. His voice was so weak that he could hardly be heard. The others helped him to his feet, but after a step or two, he fell to the ground unconscious.

Oates stayed with the sick man while Scott, Wilson, and Bowers hastened back for the sledge. He was brought to the camp unconscious, and a short time afterward, he died.

A little later, saddened by their comrade's death, the four men set out for the next depôt, which they reached without trouble.

CHAPTER XV

THE END

At the Lower Glacier Depôt, the travellers slept for five hours, worn out with the hard marches and with the shock of P. O. Evans' death. They then went on until they reached Shambles Camp, where they knew they would find food. A good supper of horse flesh put new life into the men, and they hoped to march a greater number of miles than they had done of late. But the surface was bad, and although they hauled the sledges with all their strength, they could only get on slowly.

"Pray God we get better travelling, as we are not so fit as we were, and the season is advancing apace," was the sad entry in Scott's journal.

But a few days later, he was writing with more hope. Cairns were being found with ease, and he hoped they would have no further difficulty in keeping to the track.

At the next depôt, they were disappointed because, while there was food for ten days, the measure of oil was scanty, so that it would have to be used with great care.

On and on the travellers plodded, suffering much from cold feet. They had not enough food to satisfy their hunger, and they talked now of little but the food supply.

On the 1st of March, they reached the Middle Barrier Depôt, and here, to their dismay, they again found only a small supply of oil. With the greatest care, they knew they could scarcely expect to make it last until the next depôt was reached, for it was 71 miles away. And the surface was worse than ever, so that often they could not march more than three and a half miles in four and a half hours.

Oates, too, was finding it hard work to march at all. His toes were frostbitten, and he was very lame. All of them felt the piercing winds, for their garments were worn thin. The future was dark, yet whatever these brave Englishmen felt, they showed no fear but spoke to one another as though their difficulties would soon be over.

"We mean to see the game through with a proper spirit," wrote Scott. "But it's tough work to be pulling harder than we ever pulled in our lives for long hours and to feel that the progress is so slow."

Food was again running short, yet they were

It was hardly possible after a day's march to set up the tent.

forced to keep on full rations if they were to be able to pull the sledges even a few miles.

Oates' feet had become so painful that he was now forced to sit on the sledge and allow himself to be pulled. How keenly he felt this it is easy to imagine. Yet he did not murmur; only as the days went by, he grew always a little more silent.

"The poor soldier has become a terrible hindrance," wrote Scott, but neither he nor the others let Oates see that they felt this, while they did all they could for him with great kindness. Even had Oates been well, it was now doubtful if they could have got back in safety; with one of their number ill, they had "only a dog's chance, no more."

Each day, the weather grew worse. Everything was so frozen that it was hardly possible after a day's march to set up the tent.

On the 9th of March, the travellers reached a depôt, to discover not only oil but food also short. They had hoped to find the dogs waiting for them at Mount Hooper. But Cherry-Garrard and Demetri had been delayed at One Ton Camp for four days by a blizzard, and when it was over, they dared not go on as they had only a little dog food left.

The next day, after a short march, a blizzard forced the travellers to camp. Oates was much worse, and knowing this, he asked his comrades what he should do. They urged him to go on with them as long as possible. Soon his hands and feet were so frostbitten that he could not use them, and he begged the others to leave him behind in his sleeping bag. When they still begged him to make another effort, he struggled on once more.

At night, the sick man was so weak that he believed the end had come, but morning dawned and he awoke to another day. Then he knew that he must delay no longer. A blizzard was blowing, and he said to his friends, "I am just going outside and may be some time."

They knew what would befall the sick man if he left the tent, and they begged him not to go, but undeterred by their words, he walked out into the storm, and his friends saw him no more.

"It was the act of a brave man and an English gentleman," wrote Scott. "We all hope to meet the end with a similar spirit, and assuredly the end is not far."

Serious frostbites now threatened Scott, Wilson, and Bowers. The blizzard delayed them for a day, yet still they talked to one another of "fetching through."

When only twenty-one miles from One Ton Depôt, drifting snow forced them to stop. "No human being could face it, and all are worn out nearly," was the sad record of Scott's journal.

Only a little oil, only a small quantity of spirit was now left, and while the depôt was still fifteen and a half miles away, there was food only for two days.

But the brave spirit of the men was unconquered. They struggled on until they were within eleven miles of One Ton Depôt. The next day, a blizzard made it impossible to march.

As a last chance, it was decided that Wilson and Bowers should try to reach the depôt to get food and fuel. But the storm raged so fiercely that it was useless to make the attempt.

On the 20th of March, the men had food for two days and spirit to heat two cups of tea for each. On the 22nd and 23rd, the blizzard still raged.

"We shall stick it out to the end, but we are getting weaker, of course, and the end cannot be far,"

A GREAT CAIRN WAS BUILT OVER THE TENT, AND ON

THE TOP OF THE CAIRN WAS PLACED A CROSS.

wrote Scott with unfaltering courage. Then came those last few words, "For God's sake, look after our people," which, as you know, reached the hearts of his countrymen and moved them to swift response.

Without the tent, the wind howled, the snow swirled. Within the tent had fallen the "Great Silence, the peace of the great Release."

Eight months later, a search party reached One Ton Camp, and marching eleven miles farther south, found the tent in which three men had laid down their lives. Here the diary was found which told the story of these brave men's unselfish care for their sick companions, and of their gallant fight with death.

After the burial service had been read, a great cairn was built over the tent, and on the top of the cairn was placed a cross.